The War of the Worlds

*Retold from the H. G. Wells original
by Chris Sasaki*

Illustrated by Jamel Akib

Sterling Publishing Co., Inc.
New York

Library of Congress Cataloging-in-Publication Data

Sasaki, Chris.

The war of the worlds / retold from the H. G. Wells original by Chris Sasaki ;
illustrated by Jamel Akib ; afterword by Arthur Pober.

p. cm.—(Classic starts)

Summary: An abridged version of H. G. Wells' classic science fiction tale in which, as life
on Mars becomes impossible, Martians and their terrifying machines invade the earth.

ISBN-13: 978-1-4027-3688-9

ISBN-10: 1-4027-3688-6

1. Science fiction.] I. Akib, Jamel, ill. II. Pober, Arthur. III. Wells, H. G. (Herbert
George), 1866–1946. War of the worlds. IV. Title. V. Series.

PZ7.S24864War 2007

[Fic]—dc22

2006014767

2 4 6 8 10 9 7 5 3 1

Published by Sterling Publishing Co., Inc.
387 Park Avenue South, New York, NY 10016
Copyright © 2007 by Chris Sasaki
Illustrations copyright © 2007 by Jamel Akib
c/o Canadian Manda Group, 165 Dufferin Street
Toronto, Ontario, Canada M6K 3H6
Distributed in the United Kingdom by GMC Distribution Services,
Castle Place, 166 High Street, Lewes, East Sussex, England BN7 1XU
Distributed in Australia by Capricorn Link (Australia) Pty. Ltd.
P.O. Box 704, Windsor, NSW 2756, Australia

Classic Starts is a trademark of Sterling Publishing Co., Inc.

Printed in China
All rights reserved

Sterling ISBN-13: 978-1-4027-3688-9
ISBN-10: 1-4027-3688-6

For information about custom editions, special sales, premium and
corporate purchases, please contact Sterling Special Sales
Department at 800-805-5489 or specialsales@sterlingpub.com.

CONTENTS

CHAPTER 1

The Eve of the War

At the dawn of the twentieth century, no one would have believed that the Earth was being watched by creatures smarter than we are. No one would have thought humans were being studied in the same way that we study living creatures under a microscope. We thought we were the masters of our world. But then, perhaps the tiny things under our microscopes think they are the masters of their world, too.

Who would have thought that a threat to humanity could come from another planet? Who would have thought there was even life on other planets? But creatures were watching us from across space and making their plans. And so we discovered that we are not alone and we are not the masters.

Astronomers say that Mars is older than the Earth. They also say that if life has found a home on the red planet, it must have started long before life began here. And if it started long before life on Earth, Martian creatures must be more advanced than we are.

We also know that the red planet lies farther from the light and heat of the Sun than the Earth does. In fact, no place on its surface gets warmer than our coldest winters. The air is thinner than ours, and its oceans have disappeared. Its north and south poles are covered by huge polar ice caps. Martians would need to be intelligent to survive in such a hostile environment. It's possible that the difficult conditions would have made them crueler and more willing to do anything to stay alive.

Scientists think Mars is a dying planet. Perhaps it was becoming harder for the Martians to live there. They must have looked across space and seen our planet—warm, filled with green plants and blue water, with an atmosphere full of clouds. Maybe this was how their planet had once been. Perhaps invading Earth was the only thing they could do to survive.

The Martians had probably been preparing for years. With their advanced intelligence, they built spacecraft and planned their invasion in great detail. In 1894, astronomers saw a bright light on the surface of the planet. I believe the light came from the building of a huge cannon, which they used to launch their spacecraft to Earth.

The next sign of the approaching invasion came at a time when Mars was at its closest to

Earth. At around midnight on a clear, dark night, great clouds of bright gas were seen on the planet's surface. It was as if a huge jet of flame had been shot from a cannon. The next day I happened to meet an astronomer named Ogilvy on my daily walk. He told me about the sighting and invited me to join him at his observatory after sunset.

The observatory was dark and quiet. The only light came from a small lantern. The only sound was the steady ticking of the telescope's gears. I looked through the instrument and saw Mars, a pin's head of light surrounded by the darkness of space. It seemed like such a little thing, so bright and small. Through the telescope, I could just make out markings on its surface. It lay some forty million miles from us. I understood then what few people understand—that the planets are like specks of dust floating in the vast emptiness of space.

What I could not see with the telescope was the Thing the Martians had just launched. As I would learn soon, however, the object was flying swiftly and steadily toward us. It crossed that great distance, getting closer with every minute. It was the Thing that would bring terrible destruction.

Around midnight, I saw a flash of red light coming from the planet. Ogilvy looked through the telescope and cried out. A jet of gas was being shot into space. As we would find out, it was the launch of another missile from Mars to Earth. This one had been launched only twenty-four hours after the first. Ogilvy and I watched until one in the morning, but we didn't see anything else. Finally, we closed the observatory and walked to his house. Around us, people slept peacefully in the darkness of the night.

Ogilvy didn't believe there was life on Mars. And even if there was, he explained, it was unlikely that life on two different planets would turn out the same. "The chances are a million to one that there are human-like beings on Mars," he said. Ogilvy believed that meteorites were falling on the red planet and creating explosions. Or that huge volcanoes were erupting on its surface.

The next night, another flame was seen, and again the night after that. The flames appeared for a total of ten nights. Astronomers watched as great clouds of smoke spread around the red planet, hiding its surface from view. Stories began to appear in the newspapers. Still, as the missiles rushed toward us, we carried on with our daily lives.

A few days after my night in the observatory, my wife and I went for a walk after dinner. We lived in Maybury, a small village southwest of London. From the road, we could see the lights of nearby Horsell and Woking shining across the fields. Woking was the largest town in the area, and its lights shone brightly. As we walked the country roads, I pointed out Mars to my wife. It was just a bright dot of light getting higher in the sky. Everything seemed so safe and peaceful.

CHAPTER 2

The Falling Star Lands on Horsell Common

⤳

Then came the night of the first falling star. It flashed across the sky just before dawn—a line of greenish light. Some said they heard a hissing sound as it fell. I was at home, working in my study. And although I should have seen it through my window, I saw nothing.

Ogilvy did, however, and thought a meteorite may have hit the Earth. He rose early that morning and searched the fields around Horsell. Soon after dawn, he came upon an enormous crater in a field called Horsell Common. A large object had made the hole. Sand and gravel had been scattered in every direction. Bushes were on fire, smoke rose into the dawn sky, and the ground was burned black as far as you could see.

The Thing lay nearly buried in the sand. It was still so hot from its fall from space that Ogilvy could not get close. But he was near enough to see the part sticking out of the ground. It was shaped like a cylinder and measured about thirty yards across. As the astronomer stood there, he heard a faint noise from within the object. He knew then that it wasn't a meteorite that had plunged from the sky.

Ash began to fall from the end of the cylinder in flakes. Ogilvy climbed down into the pit to take a closer look at the Thing and saw that the ash was coming loose because the top of the cylinder was turning very slowly. It was then that he realized the object was hollow. Something inside was unscrewing the top!

"There's a man in it!" he said out loud. "Half roasted to death! Trying to escape!" He tried to get closer, but the heat still kept him from approaching. So he climbed out of the pit and ran to Woking. He asked the people he met for help, but no one believed his story. At last, he saw someone he knew—a man named Henderson—standing in his garden.

"Henderson," cried Ogilvy, "did you see the shooting star last night? It's fallen on Horsell Common."

"A fallen meteorite?" Henderson asked.

"Not a meteorite," explained the astronomer. "It's a cylinder! And there's something inside!"

Soon Henderson and Ogilvy were standing at the edge of the crater looking at the Thing. The sound coming from inside had stopped. There was a space between the top of the cylinder and the main part. The two men could hear air being sucked through the gap. The object had finally cooled enough that they could get closer, so they climbed down into the hole. They rapped on the cylinder's surface with a stick but heard nothing. The man or men inside must be dead, they thought. There was nothing more that the astronomer and his companion could do, so the pair hurried back to town for help. Henderson worked for a newspaper in London. He went to the railway station to telegraph the news to them so that everyone would hear about the cylinder.

By eight o'clock that morning, people from town were making their way to the pit to see the "dead men from Mars." I didn't find out what was happening until I heard about it from a newspaper boy. When I did, I set out right away to see the cylinder for myself.

By the time I arrived, a small crowd of people had gathered. They were looking at the object in silence. I climbed down into the huge hole for a closer look.

As I stood studying the strange cylinder, many thoughts ran through my mind. I was sure it had come from Mars. I believed there were men on the red planet, but I didn't think the cylinder contained living creatures. After all, unscrewing the top could simply be the work of a machine. Still, I wanted to see it open. Perhaps it contained unearthly devices or books that we could translate. I waited around until eleven that morning, but nothing more happened, so I walked back home.

By the time I returned to the common that afternoon, word of the crash had spread. Newspapers contained stories about the cylinder with headlines like A MESSAGE RECEIVED FROM MARS. People had come from nearby towns and formed a large crowd around the crater. It was a hot day, without a cloud in the sky. Someone was selling apples and beverages from a cart. I saw Henderson, Ogilvy, and another astronomer—a man named Stent. The cylinder had cooled and Stent was standing on it. He was yelling to a number of workers with shovels and pickaxes. They had uncovered more of the object. The men tried to open it, but with no luck.

The afternoon passed and the cylinder remained closed. I went home to eat and to give my wife the latest news about the Thing from Mars.

CHAPTER 3

The Cylinder and the Heat-Ray

I returned to the pit just as the sun was setting. Two or three hundred people now surrounded the crater. They were yelling and pushing one another for a better view. Over the noise, I heard Stent's voice. "Keep back! Keep back! We don't know what's in it," he cried.

A boy came running toward me. "It's moving!" he said as he sped past. "It's opening. I don't like it. I'm going home."

I made my way through the crowd and saw a young man standing on the Thing. I also saw that the end of it was still turning. The gap between the top and the rest of the cylinder was now nearly two feet. Suddenly the top fell and landed on the ground with a heavy thud. The young man was startled and fell into the pit. A great silence came over the crowd.

The inside of the cylinder was dark. As my eyes became used to the blackness, I saw shadowy shapes moving within. Two eyes looked out at me from the gloomy depths. Then something that looked like a small gray snake came into sight.

A chill came over me. A woman in the crowd screamed. I could see that the "snake" was actually a tentacle. As more tentacles slithered out of the darkness, I moved away from the edge of the pit. The surprised looks on people's faces turned to looks of horror. The crowd backed away from the Thing. Some—including Stent turned and ran.

A large, gray, round body slowly slid into view on the lip of the cylinder. It shone like wet leather. Two large, dark eyes stared out at us. Under the eyes, a quivering mouth dripped a liquid of some kind. Two clusters of tentacles grew from either side of the mouth. One tentacle gripped the edge of the cylinder while another waved in the air.

The creature looked horrible and strange. Its mouth was V-shaped, and it had a pointed upper

lip. The creature's skin was brown and oily. Its gigantic eyes were dark and frightening. As I looked at the Martian, I was filled with dread.

Suddenly the creature slid over the edge of the cylinder and fell into the pit with a wet thud. Another Martian appeared from within, and I heard the first one cry out. It was then that I turned and ran toward some trees. I took cover and looked around. People were huddled in ditches, behind bushes, and behind gates, in a great circle around the pit. They were all watching in horror. A man standing near me was repeating out loud, but to no one in particular, "What ugly brutes! What ugly brutes!" The young man who had fallen into the pit was trying to climb out. Suddenly he slipped back into the hole with a loud yell. I was too afraid to help him.

As scared as I was, I also wanted to get a closer look at the Martians. I began walking around the cylinder, searching for a better view. I saw the creatures' tentacles whip the air. As I crept along, a thin rod rose up from within the pit. At the end of the rod, a shiny, circular disk spun around and around.

I found a small hill that gave me a better view and waited there. Everything was silent, so people moved closer. Three policemen—one riding a horse—tried to control the crowd and keep them at a safe distance.

A small group of men—including Henderson, Stent, and Ogilvy—began walking toward the pit. One of them was waving a white flag. It looked to me as if they were going to try to talk with the creatures.

As the men approached, a bright light flashed from within the hole. Greenish smoke clouded the air and a hissing sound cut through the silence of the common. A dome-shaped object slowly rose from the depths. A beam of light flickered from it.

Flames burst out all around the three men, and they fell to the ground. It was as if the fire had sprung from a beam or ray I couldn't see. Beyond where the men had been standing, trees and bushes erupted into flame as the invisible ray of heat reached them. The windows and brick walls of nearby sheds exploded. I heard the crackle of fire as the beam swept around swiftly and steadily like a sword of heat.

I could see that the Heat-Ray was swinging closer to me. More and more nearby bushes caught fire. Then, suddenly, the hissing stopped and the dome-shaped object sank back out of sight.

The fields were black. There were patches of burned bushes and trees all around me. The houses toward Woking sent flames into the still evening air. The mounted policeman galloped by with his hands over his head. He was screaming as he rode past. A woman shrieked, "They're coming!" Others, some with hats and clothing on fire, ran like a frightened flock of sheep.

I crouched as low as I could, amazed at what I had just seen. I could only guess how the Martians' Heat-Ray worked. It looked as if the domelike object was the energy source. It must somehow direct a beam of pure heat to the spinning, circular mirror. The mirror must then direct the beam the way we shine a beam of light from a lantern.

After some time passed, I realized that I was alone, helpless, and unprotected. Horsell Common was dark under the twilight sky. Overhead, the stars were appearing. I suddenly felt very scared. I turned and ran from the pit in a panic. I was afraid that the Heat-Ray would leap from the pit and strike me down at any second.

CHAPTER 4

How I Reached Home Friday Night

⌒

I ran until I could run no farther. Exhausted, I lay down by the side of the road and rested until my terror left me. I was dazed and wondered if the attack had just been a bad dream.

I got up and crossed a bridge over the canal. In the distance, a train sped through the night. I came upon a group of people on their evening walk. They were talking as if nothing had happened. I asked them if they had heard what was taking place on Horsell Common. They hadn't, and they laughed at me as if I were crazy.

I had seen the horror with my own eyes, but clearly no one more than a few miles from the pit knew what was taking place. Even people who had heard about the cylinder but hadn't been to the common didn't know that the terror had begun. The newspaper Henderson worked for hadn't believed his telegram and had decided not to report on the coming of the Thing. Passengers on local trains could see lights flickering in the direction of the pit, but most went on with their lives as if nothing were happening.

I kept walking until, finally, I reached home. My wife was shocked to see me covered in dirt and ash. She was even more surprised to see the look of terror on my face. I told her everything as I ate some dinner and regained my strength.

To make us both feel better, I told my wife what Ogilvy had said to me the other night in his observatory. The Earth's gravity, the astronomer had explained, is three times stronger than the gravity of Mars. This means that a Martian would weigh three times more on Earth than on its home planet. Because of this great weight, the Martian would have a lot of trouble moving about. "We are very lucky," I said, "that they move so slowly and with so much difficulty. I don't see how they could even get out of the pit. But still, they're horrible creatures."

By the time I had finished eating, I didn't feel the same fear I had felt before. "One direct hit from a cannon will kill them all," I said bravely. I didn't know it then, but I was like a bird saying, *We have nothing to fear from those hunters and their guns!*

Perhaps feeling the same sense of bravery as I did, many of the people who had run from the Heat-Ray ignored the danger and returned to the edge of the common. They were hoping to see what would happen next. A few people even tried to get another look and crawled closer to the pit. But each time someone approached, a searchlight would shine from the cylinder, followed by the ray. None of those foolhardy souls was ever seen again.

Then the Martians began to build their machines. Puffs of green-white smoke and the sound of hammering emerged from the pit. At eleven o'clock that night, a group of soldiers arrived and positioned themselves around the invaders. At midnight, the crowd huddled around the common saw a green star fall from the sky and land in the woods nearby. It lit up the heavens as it went. It was the second cylinder.

CHAPTER 5

The Fighting Begins

⁓

I had difficulty sleeping and rose early on Saturday morning. Outside, I saw the milkman and asked if he'd heard any news. He told me that troops had surrounded the Martians during the night and that the artillery was on its way. I also saw my neighbor and talked with him. He was sure the soldiers would capture or destroy the Martians that very day. "It's too bad," he said. "It would be interesting to learn how they live." Then he told me that another object had fallen from the sky.

After breakfast, I decided to walk down to the common. But when I came to the canal, a group of soldiers told me that no one was allowed to cross the bridge. They had been ordered to keep people away from the cylinder. They had also been instructed to make everyone leave Horsell.

I told them what I had seen the night before, and we began to argue about the best way to destroy the monsters. Then I described the creatures to them. "They must look like octopuses," said one of the soldiers with a mixture of fear and disgust.

Seeing the army in place, I began to feel better. The Martians moved slowly and helplessly in their pit. I felt confident that we could kill them easily. Sure enough, at three o'clock I heard the sound of a distant cannon. The military was trying to destroy the second cylinder before it opened.

I returned home to wait for news. Around six o'clock that evening, my wife and I heard explosions coming from where the first cylinder lay. The thunderous sounds were followed by a loud crash that shook the ground. We ran to the front of the house just in time to see the tops of nearby trees burst into flame. A large brick building in the village crumbled before our eyes. The tower of a church collapsed and slid to the ground. The chimney of our house exploded as if it had been hit by a shell. The pieces came crashing down around our feet.

My wife and I were stunned. It was then that I realized we were in danger from the Heat-Ray. With the large buildings of Maybury gone, there was nothing standing between us and instant death.

"We can't stay here," I shouted.

"But where can we go?" my wife cried in terror.

"To my cousins in Leatherhead," I said. I left her behind the safety of a stone fence and ran to the Spotted Dog, an inn not far from our home. Once there, I got the landlord to lend me a small horse-drawn wagon. I promised I would return it and drove back to my home. While my wife waited outside, I rushed into the house to gather some belongings.

As I came back outside, a soldier rushed by warning people to leave. "What's happening?" I shouted to him.

As he ran, he turned and yelled, ". . . crawling out of the pit in a thing like a metal shield . . ."

The soldier disappeared into a cloud of black smoke that whirled across the road. I finished loading the wagon and helped my wife into her seat. Then I climbed in and grabbed the reins, and we headed down the road.

In front of us, the sun shone on quiet wheat fields. Behind us there was fire and great, boiling clouds of black smoke. People ran along the roads, fleeing from the alien attackers. I hurried in the direction of Leatherhead, not slowing until Horsell Common was far behind us.

We arrived in Leatherhead at about nine o'clock, and I told my cousins all that had happened. My wife was very worried, so I reminded her of the Martians' weakness at moving about. It did little to comfort her, however, and she begged me to stay in Leatherhead. But I had promised the innkeeper that I would return his wagon. And to be honest, I wanted to see the battle. As strange as it sounds, I was afraid that the last explosions we heard had signaled the destruction of the invaders and that I had missed it.

It was nearly eleven o'clock by the time I was ready to return to Maybury. My wife stood in the light of the doorway as I jumped into the wagon. As I set off, she turned and disappeared inside.

The night was black, but I knew the way. To the west, I could see shadowy clouds of a thunderstorm as well as great columns of black-and-red smoke. I passed dark, quiet houses. I didn't know whether the people inside were asleep or had left their homes to escape the Martians. There was a group of people standing quietly along the road. They were looking in the direction of the common. I wasn't far from Maybury when I heard the bells of a distant church marking midnight.

Just then a bright glow lit up the countryside. A streak of unearthly green cut through the clouds and fell into the field to my left. It was the third falling star!

This strange sight was followed by the first lightning flashes from the gathering storm. The thunderclaps sounded as if they'd come from a gigantic machine. As a light hail began to fall, my horse bolted down the road. It was then that I saw something moving quickly down the side of a hill. At first it looked like the wet roof of a house. Then there was a great flash of lightning and I saw it more clearly.

How can I describe this thing? It looked like a giant three-legged machine—a tripod contraption taller than a house with great metal cables dangling from it. It was like a walking engine of glittering metal. It kept knocking down trees as it crossed the fields.

As I watched in amazement, a second tripod-machine crashed through the woods in front of me. It looked like a man stepping through tall grass. The machine was headed right for me. I pulled hard on the reins to turn the horse and wagon around. But I pulled too hard, and the horse went down. The wagon flew over the horse and I was thrown into a shallow pool of water by the side of the road.

I scrambled out of the water and under a bush just as the giant marched past me. It was an eerie

sight. A metal hood sat on three legs. It turned back and forth like the head of a person looking first one way and then the other. What I had thought were cables were actually long mechanical tentacles. The machine coughed out great green clouds that trailed behind it like smoke from a speeding train. Behind the hood was a metal basket like the kind a fisherman would use to hold his catch.

As the machine passed, it let out a deafening howl—*Aloo! Aloo!* The cry was even louder than the thunder. In no time at all, the tripod was standing in a field with the first machine. The two were bent over as if looking at something on the ground between them. I have no doubt they were looking at the third cylinder.

I lay in the rain for a while, watching the monstrous machines moving in the distance. Finally, the shock of seeing them wore off and I struggled to my feet. Careful not to be seen, I ran to a nearby hut. It was locked, so I crawled into a ditch and followed it to the pine woods. Wet, tired, and cold, I stumbled through the trees until I came upon a road. I followed the road in the rain until I reached home. I opened the front door, staggered in, and sat down at the bottom of the staircase. In my mind, I could still see those towering metal monsters marching through the darkness.

CHAPTER 6

The Artilleryman

Sitting on the floor, I felt wet and chilled. I got up, found something to drink, and changed into dry clothes. From my study upstairs, I looked out the window and saw that the thunderstorm had passed. The sky was clear, and Mars was setting in the west.

I saw the work of the Heat-Ray everywhere I looked. In Woking, piles of rubble sat where buildings had once stood. A wrecked train burned on the tracks near the station. The streets were empty except for people scurrying from hiding place to hiding place. It was hard to imagine that this was the peaceful world I had lived in for so many years.

It seemed as if the whole countryside was on fire. In the distance, the field around the Martians' pit glowed with a red light. Against this glare, three huge, black shapes moved about.

As I sat looking out my study window, I began to wonder about the giant machines. Were they intelligent mechanical monsters? Or did a Martian sit inside each one, controlling it the way our brain controls our body? I was overcome by the feeling that I was like an animal wondering how a train or a steamship worked.

Just then I saw a soldier climb the fence into my garden. I leaned out the window and got his attention with a whisper.

"Where are you going?" I asked.

"I don't know," was his reply. "I'm trying to hide."

"Then come into the house," I said.

I went downstairs, unlocked the door, and let him in. "What happened?" I asked once the man was inside.

"They wiped us out. Simply wiped us out," he explained as he sat down at the table. He laid his head on his arms and began to cry.

After a few minutes, the soldier calmed himself and explained that he was with the artillery. He told me the Martians had crawled from the first cylinder and crossed the field to the second cylinder under some sort of metal shield. The army fired at them, but then the shield rose up on three legs. This was one of the tripod-machines I had seen. As it walked across the field, the machine raised its Heat-Ray.

The artilleryman had been setting up his gun when his horse had stepped in a hole and he was thrown into a ditch. It was at this moment that the Heat-Ray struck. The gun exploded behind him and the shells blew up in a blaze of flame. He was the only one of his unit to survive.

The artilleryman told me that he lay in the ditch for a long time. From his hiding place, he saw the giant turn its Heat-Ray on Woking and destroy the entire town. Then it turned and headed to the smoking woods where the second cylinder had fallen.

A second tripod-machine appeared and followed the first. When it seemed safe, the artilleryman had hurried away toward what was left of Woking. He came across a ditch by the side of the road and crawled along it until he reached town. There were crumbling, burning buildings everywhere, but very few people to be seen. Suddenly one of the Martian machines appeared again. The artilleryman hid. He waited until the invader had gone and then made his way through the ruins from Woking to Maybury. Finally he reached my home.

After we both ate, we went upstairs to my study and looked out at the towns and fields. The countryside was scorched as far as the eye could see. Very little had escaped the Heat-Ray. Against the faint light of the sky, we saw the fighting-machines standing near the second pit. Their heads turned as if they were keeping watch, and green puffs of smoke rose up around them.

CHAPTER 7

Destruction on the River Thames

༄

As the dawn grew brighter, the artilleryman and I decided that it wasn't safe to stay in the house. He said he was going to London to get new orders. I decided that I would go to Leatherhead to find my wife. After what I had seen, I knew that the only safe thing to do would be to leave the country. But the third cylinder lay between us, so my companion convinced me to go with him instead. Once I was far enough north, I would be able to turn and make my way east toward Leatherhead.

The artilleryman and I went through every room and gathered food and water for our journey. Then we crept out of the house. We ran as quickly and quietly as we could. The houses we passed were dark and deserted. In the road, people had dropped belongings as they fled—a clock, a slipper, a silver spoon, and other valuables littered the street. A wagon had tipped over at a crossroads and spilled boxes and furniture onto the ground. But we saw no one. Everyone must have either escaped or gone into hiding.

It was a quiet morning. The artilleryman and I stopped to listen once or twice, but we didn't hear anything. Even the birds were silent. At last, the stillness was broken by the sound of horses. We saw three soldiers riding slowly toward Woking and called to them to stop. One was a lieutenant, who asked us what we knew.

"My gun was destroyed last night, sir," explained the artilleryman. "We've been hiding ever since. I'm heading to London to rejoin my company. You'll see the Martians if you follow this road for half a mile."

"What are they like?" the lieutenant asked.

"Giants in armor," my companion replied. "A hundred feet tall. Three legs and a metal body, with a mighty head on top."

"What nonsense!" the lieutenant cried out.

"And they carry some kind of box that shoots fire," continued the artilleryman. "A Heat-Ray."

"Well, we'll see for ourselves," said the lieutenant. "Look here, we're clearing people out of their houses. You'd better go along and report to Brigadier General Marvin. Tell him all you know. He's in Weybridge, on your way to London."

The soldiers turned their horses south and rode off toward Woking. We never saw them again.

As we made our way north, we came upon a group of soldiers standing guard on a bridge. In a nearby field, six large cannons sat pointing in the direction from which we had just come.

"That's good," I said. "At least they'll get one good shot in."

"They're like bows and arrows against lightning," said the artilleryman. "They're no use against the Heat-Ray."

We continued on and came to a small town where the roads were noisy and crowded. Soldiers were riding about on horseback, urgently telling everyone to leave all their belongings. But the people were ignoring the warnings and packing crates and furniture onto wagons. I saw an old man carrying a huge box and an armful of orchids in flowerpots. I stopped him and grabbed his arm. "Do you know what's over there?" I said angrily. I pointed toward the trees that hid the Martians.

"But I can't leave these behind," he replied.

"Death!" I shouted. "Death is over there!" I left him and hurried to catch up with the artilleryman. When I looked back, I saw the old man standing with his box and flowers staring helplessly over the trees.

Finally we reached Weybridge. It was even noisier and more crowded than the last town. Carts, carriages, and horses choked the roadways. People loaded their families and baggage into wagons. Here, too, soldiers were telling people to leave or to hide in their cellars as soon as the fighting began. A crowd was gathering at the railway station. The platform was piled with boxes and packages, but there were no trains. They were being used to carry soldiers and weapons.

No one could tell us where to find Brigadier General Marvin, so the artilleryman and I walked to the docks where the ferry crossed the River Thames. Dozens of boats crowded the river. A growing, noisy group of people milled restlessly around the docks. They were carrying their boxes and bags with them in the hope of finding a boat that would take them downriver to London. One husband and wife carried a small door between them. It was piled high with household goods. It was clear from what many in the crowd were saying that they still thought the Martians would be defeated. There was no panic yet, but there were already too many people and not enough boats.

Suddenly someone cried out above the noise of the crowd, "What's that?" Everyone fell silent and we heard a thud from somewhere to the west. It was the sound of a gun. The gunshot was followed by more blasts from another direction. The Martians were on the move. The fighting had begun again.

Far upriver, a puff of smoke rose into the air. Then we heard a huge explosion that shook the ground and broke windows. "There they are!" a man shouted. "Do you see them? There!"

The Martians appeared to the west, far beyond the trees. Five of the metal fighting-machines were heading toward the river. They shone in the morning sun as they moved closer and closer.

The sight of these strange and terrible things filled the crowd with horror. They stood in silence. Then they began to move. They pushed past me, slowly at first, then faster and faster. I turned to flee.

One of the fighting-machines lifted something above its head. Suddenly the Heat-Ray flashed through the air. "Get under the water!" I shouted to any who would listen. I rushed down to the riverbank and ran in. A few others followed.

The Martian machine got closer. But instead of attacking us, it waded into the Thames. In no time at all, it was halfway to the other side. At that moment, six guns began firing from their hiding place on the far side of the river. The monster was just about to unleash the Heat-Ray when the first shell exploded above its head. Two more shells burst nearby. Finally, a fourth shell found its target. Flames and metal flew into the air.

"Hit!" I shouted. The crippled machine wobbled on its legs, but it did not fall down. Even though the Martian inside must have been killed, it kept walking unsteadily. The Thing staggered out of the river and into the town on the other side. It crashed into a church and smashed the tower. Then it stumbled backward and fell into the river with a huge explosion. Water and metal shot far up into the sky. The Heat-Ray turned the river into a boiling frenzy. Thick clouds of steam swirled through the air. Metal tentacles waved wildly, sending water and mud flying everywhere. The crippled fighting-machine looked like a wounded animal struggling for its life.

Just then a man shouted and pointed behind me. I turned and saw the other Martian machines heading toward us along the riverbank. I dove under the water and held my breath as long as I could. When I finally raised my head into the air, the steam rising off the river was hiding everything from sight.

The mist cleared for a moment and I spotted the four Martians near the far riverbank. Two were leaning over their destroyed comrade. Two more were standing close by, sending their Heat-Rays in all directions.

The noise was deafening—the howl of the Martians, the crash of falling houses, the burning trees. Black smoke mixed with the steam from the river. As the Heat-Rays swept through the air, houses, fences, and sheds burst into flames.

The mob around me scrambled out of the water like frogs scurrying from the feet of an approaching human. Suddenly the Heat-Rays swept across the river and toward us. As I ran to shore, a huge wave of boiling water washed over me. I struggled to the riverbank and fell to the ground. I could see the Martians returning to this side of the river and thought it was the end.

A giant metal foot came down not far from where I lay. I looked up and watched as the four fighting-machines, carrying the wreckage of the fifth, disappeared into the steam and smoke. Somehow I had escaped.

CHAPTER 8

How I Met the Curate

∽

Now that we had destroyed one of their machines, the Martians knew we were not completely helpless. They quickly retreated to Horsell Common and the first cylinder. This may be why they paid no attention to me lying on the river-bank, and why so many others escaped. Perhaps they were more concerned with the attack and the damaged fighting-machine than with the humans running about in a panic at their feet. Or maybe that is wishful thinking. Perhaps we escaped because they were simply not worried about us. After all, another cylinder arrived each day, and their strength was quickly growing.

Whatever the reason, they returned to the pit and gave the army time to put more guns in place. The artillery was hidden behind every hill and in every forest and village in the Martians' path.

The halt in the battle also let the soldiers take up positions from which they could watch the creatures more closely. From their lookout posts, the soldiers saw the monsters move everything from the second and third cylinders to the first. Then, while a single creature stood guard, the Martians crawled from their tripod-machines and down into the pit. As they began to work, clouds of thick green smoke rose into the dark sky.

While the Martians and the army prepared for the next battle, I tried to get as far from the fire and panic of Weybridge as possible. The artillery-man and I had lost each other in the confusion of the attack. I was now alone. I saw a boat drifting downstream. I thought it would be safer to be near water in case the creatures and the Heat-Ray returned, so I swam to the boat and climbed in. It had no oars, so I paddled with my hands. I headed downriver in the direction of London.

But I was exhausted and my hands were burned from the boiling water, so I soon stopped paddling and drifted with the current. I passed through a town and saw that it was empty. Many of the houses near the river were on fire. I became afraid and started paddling again. When my hunger finally became overpowering and the afternoon sun too intense, I made my way to shore. I climbed out of the boat and walked until I found a shaded spot by a hedge. I lay down there and soon fell asleep.

When I awoke, it was nearly sunset. A man was sitting next to me. "Do you have any water?" I asked.

He shook his head without looking at me. "No. You've been asking for water for the last hour." His clothes were covered in soot. He had large eyes that stared into the distance.

"What happened?" he asked. "Why has this happened? This morning, everything was normal. And now everything has been wiped out! Why?"

I could see that the coming of the Martians had greatly disturbed him. I wanted to help, but I had no answers to his questions. All I could do was talk to the man. As we spoke, he calmed down and told me about himself.

"I'm a curate," he explained. "A priest. I've come to work at the local church."

"You must keep your head," I said. "There is still hope."

He continued to stare off into the distance. "It's the beginning of the end," he said. "How can we escape? They can't be defeated."

"But I saw one killed this afternoon," I replied.

Just then we heard the booming of far-off guns followed by a strange crying sound. "Listen," I said. I pointed to the southwest. "The Martians are in that direction." Then I pointed toward London. "And in that direction, the army is putting guns in place. We're right in the middle. It won't be long before the fighting-machines come this way. We had better go."

CHAPTER 9

The March Toward London

‿∽

The Martians truly began their attack on Sunday evening. At eight o'clock, three of the fighting-machines appeared from the pit on Horsell Common. They spread out in a line, each about a mile and a half apart. Then they started signaling to one another with haunting, siren-like howls. Suddenly the line of machines began their march toward the waiting artillery.

When the Martians reached the first set of guns, they were greeted with a burst of cannon fire. But after firing once, the soldiers were overcome with fear at the sight of the approaching enemy and quickly fled on horseback or on foot. The Martians swept right past the deserted positions.

Farther on, the invaders came upon more soldiers hidden in the forest. The soldiers began to fire at the closest of the attackers. The shells flashed all around it. The machine took a few steps, staggered, and then fell to the ground. The soldiers cheered as they reloaded.

One of the legs of the fallen fighting-machine had been smashed. It lay on the ground signaling loudly, and the other two metallic giants quickly appeared. The guns fired again, but this time they missed their targets. The two Martians turned their Heat-Rays on the artillery, and the trees around the guns burst into flame. The unfired shells lying on the ground exploded. The soldiers who weren't killed instantly fled over the top of a hill.

With grasping tentacles, a Martian slowly pulled itself out of the wreckage of the fallen fighting-machine. While its companions stood guard, it worked on the damaged leg. It didn't take long for the creature to finish its repair. Soon all three machines were marching across the countryside again.

At nine o'clock, four more Martians joined the first three. The new arrivals each carried a large black tube. They walked over to their three comrades and handed each of them their own tubes. The seven machines then formed a long line across the countryside and began to march.

The curate and I watched as two of them crossed the river toward us. My nervous companion let out a cry and began to run. I knew I couldn't outrun the fighting-machines, so I took cover under a bush at the side of the road. The curate looked back, saw what I was doing, and joined me.

The Martians, who had been signaling loudly to one another, stopped their advance and fell silent. They stood and waited in a long line. Hidden behind hills, trees, and houses, the soldiers and their guns also waited. The Martians and the humans faced each other beneath the darkening sky. They were both ready to do battle.

As I lay hidden, I wondered again about the invaders. What did they know about us, I asked myself. Did they understand that we were intelligent creatures who would fight back with guns and machines? Or were we nothing more to them than a swarm of bees defending a hive? I wondered if their plan was to rid the Earth of humans completely. If so, did we have any chance of stopping them?

My thoughts were interrupted by what sounded like a far-off gunshot. This was followed by another, then another. The Martian near us raised his tube into the air and fired it like a gun.

The loud explosion shook the ground. We heard yet another shot in the distance. Then, after a final blast, I saw something like a shell from a cannon flying through the air far above me.

The countryside briefly fell silent, and then I heard the distant sound of shouting. As quickly as it started, the shouting stopped and there was silence again. I expected to hear the hidden artillery come to life, but there was nothing.

The Martian towering above us marched off into the darkness. I crawled from my hiding place, clambered up a small cliff, and looked around. To the east I saw what looked like two black clouds. They continued to grow slowly as I watched. To the north I saw a third cloud. Far away to the southwest, the curate and I could hear the Martians calling to one another. This was followed by the thud of their tube-guns. I expected to hear the sound of our artillery answer back, but there was still no reply.

As I later found out, the Martians used the black tubes to fire large shells. It was one of these shells that I had seen flying through the air. When they hit the ground, the shells released a heavy, black gas. The gas floated down hills, ran through ditches, and flowed along streets like a river that had flooded its banks. It was poisonous and killed anyone and anything that breathed it in. After a while, the cloud sank to the ground like dust, and the Martians could clear it away using a giant jet of steam.

With the Martians gone for the moment, the curate and I found shelter in a deserted house. From there we watched as searchlights criss-crossed the sky. We heard the sound of guns echoing across the fields. Then the searchlights disappeared and were replaced by a bright red glow. The guns fell silent, and all was still.

Like a farmer smoking out a wasps' nest, the Martians spread their black clouds as they made their way to London. They launched shells of gas before our guns even had a chance to fire. Where our soldiers were out in the open, they used their Heat-Rays.

As the Martians marched along the ground, another green streak flashed overhead. It was the fourth cylinder.

And so Sunday night marked the end of any real chance at stopping the invasion. Soldiers standing ready with their artillery never had a chance to fire. The Martians' shells exploded around them, releasing a swift, choking blackness that spared no one. The gunboats that had steamed up the River Thames were useless, and the crews left their posts in the face of an unbeatable foe.

CHAPTER 10

In London

⁓

I saw the first Martians crawl from their cylinder and unleash their Heat-Ray on Friday. On Saturday, I saw the fighting-machines cross the fields for the first time. And on Sunday, I saw the attack on Weybridge and watched the Martians begin their march toward London.

My younger brother lived in London and didn't see any of this. He could only read about it in the newspapers or listen to people's stories as they flooded into the city.

He didn't hear about the cylinder falling on Horsell Common until the day after it happened. The stories about Mars and about the object that had crashed to Earth first appeared in Saturday's papers. They explained that the Martians had killed a number of people, but probably could not climb out of their pit because of the Earth's strong gravity. It didn't sound too serious, so my brother wasn't terribly worried about me. Still, he decided to travel to Maybury to see the Martians before they were killed. When he went to the train station, however, he was told that the trains were not running from that part of the country. Apparently, there had been some sort of accident near Woking. And so he remained in London.

Then on Sunday, an article appeared in the papers describing the events of the night before: "At seven o'clock on Saturday night, the Martians came out of their cylinder. They moved about under metals shields, wrecking Woking station and killing a unit of soldiers. No further details are known . . ."

Most people in London were still acting as if nothing unusual had happened, but my brother was becoming more worried. He went to the train station again and discovered that not only had more trains stopped running, but some of the telegraph lines were dead as well. My brother heard that fighting had begun and that people were leaving their homes and fleeing to London. Whatever trouble had started, it was growing larger and getting closer.

One or two trains came in from just outside London. The passengers said they had heard guns firing. Some had talked to soldiers who told them to escape to the city because the Martians were coming. At five o'clock, a train passed through carrying soldiers and large cannons. Shortly after that, the police arrived and ordered everyone to leave the station.

The sun was setting as my brother returned to the streets. He crossed Waterloo Bridge, where he saw a curious brown scum floating on the surface of the Thames. Then he came upon some young boys selling newspapers. They were yelling: "Fighting at Weybridge! Attack of the Martians! London in danger!" He bought a paper and read his first description of the invaders. They weren't just small, sluggish creatures, he learned. They moved swiftly over the countryside in their machines and used their Heat-Rays to destroy our guns. The paper described "huge, spiderlike machines a hundred feet high that moved as fast as an express train and shot out beams of intense heat." He read about the five that I had seen walking in the river and about the one machine that had been destroyed. As he read about the many soldiers who had been killed and the guns that had been destroyed, he began to understand the full power and terror of these monsters.

But the reports did not say things were hopeless. He read that the Martians had returned to their pit and that our forces were advancing from all sides. Guns were moving into position to defend London, and the army would try to destroy any new cylinders before they opened. Yes, the Martians were strange and horrible creatures, but there were only twenty or so of them against all of humanity.

In Trafalgar Square, my brother saw more and more people who had fled the countryside for the safety of the city. He saw a man, his wife, and two boys riding in a cart filled with furniture. Behind them was a hay wagon with five or six people in it, along with boxes and bundles. They all looked tired and worried. Many complained that the government and military were not doing all they could to destroy the invaders. The police were out in full force in the streets. Groups of people stood on the corners reading newspapers and talking with great excitement. By night, the roadways were packed.

My brother tried to find out what had happened in the area around Woking. One man told him the town had been destroyed. "I wasn't far from there," he explained. "When I looked toward Woking, all I could see was smoke. Then we heard guns, so I locked up my house and came to London."

After an evening of worry and wandering the streets, my brother finally went home and went to bed. There was nothing else he could do. But his sleep was soon interrupted by the sounds of people running in the streets, yelling, and knocking on doors. He jumped out of bed and ran to the window. When he stuck his head out, he saw people rushing from their homes. A policeman was hammering on door after door shouting, "They're coming! The Martians are coming!"

Church bells began to ring, doors slammed, and dark windows lit up. A horse-drawn carriage came clattering up the street. It was followed by other carriages and wagons. Everyone was making their way to the train station.

Just then the door to my brother's room burst open. His neighbor from across the hall ran in yelling, "What is it? A fire? What's going on?" They looked out the window and saw more and more people spilling onto the streets. The voices of newspaper sellers rang out above the noise: "London in danger! Kingston and Richmond defenses defeated! Martians attack along River Thames!"

Fear swept through the streets. London had calmly gone to bed on Sunday night and, in the early hours of Monday morning, had woken up in peril. It was the dawn of the great panic.

My brother dressed and ran outside. He bought a newspaper and read: "The Martians use rockets to spread large clouds of poisonous black smoke. They are using these deadly clouds to defeat our artillery and soldiers. They are now making their way to London. It is impossible to stop them. They are destroying everything."

All six million people who lived in London now knew what was happening outside the city. As the dawn sky grew brighter, they began to pour northward and eastward—away from the attackers. My brother returned to his room, put all his money in his pockets, and left his home.

CHAPTER 11

The Flight from London

༄

A great wave of fear swept through London in the early hours of Monday morning. People swarmed the railway stations looking for a way out of the city, but it quickly became impossible to board the packed trains. Fighting broke out, and many people were injured as the mobs tried desperately to flee. Engine drivers and crews fearing for their lives refused to return to London.

Boat docks along the Thames were just as packed. As the day went on, police lost control of the crowds. More and more people flooded onto every road that led north or east. They all wanted to get away from the Martians. At midday, a fighting-machine appeared on the outskirts of the city and let loose a great cloud of black smoke. It drifted along the river and made it impossible to cross many of the bridges leading out of the city.

After trying to board a train without success, my brother found himself on a road leading out of the city. He passed an abandoned shop and took a bicycle from its window. He slowly made his way north along a road filled with people on foot, on horseback, or driving in motorcars. When the wheel of the bicycle broke, he continued on foot. He decided to make his way to the home of some friends who lived east of London.

My brother hadn't gone far when he heard two women screaming. He hurried around a corner and saw three men. Two of them were trying to drag a dark-haired woman from a small horse-drawn carriage. The third man was holding on to the woman's horse. The dark-haired woman had a whip in her hand and was lashing out at one of the men who had grabbed her arm.

My brother quickly ran to help the women. One of the men turned toward him, but my brother easily knocked him to the ground. He tried to grab the second man, but the man ran off down the lane. The third man let go of the horse, and the wagon sped away. My brother knocked the third man to the ground.

Then, seeing his chance, my brother turned and ran after the carriage. On his way, he stumbled. When he got up again, two of the men had caught up with him. Just then the dark-haired woman came running to his rescue. She was carrying a piece of wood she had found on the ground. The men quickly turned and ran away.

My brother and the dark-haired woman rejoined the second woman in the carriage, and the three rode off. They wanted to put as much distance between them and the three men as possible. My brother learned that the dark-haired woman who had saved him was named Miss Elphinstone. The other woman was her sister-in-law. She was married to Miss Elphinstone's older brother. The three of them lived together, not far from London. The husband had awakened the two women the night before, packed them into the carriage, and told them to drive to the train station and wait for him. He told his wife that he would catch up to them in the morning. They would take a train together then. But the husband never showed up, and the women could not stay at the train station. The crowd was becoming too large and dangerous, so they left on their own.

My brother told the women of his own escape from London. Then the three of them talked about what to do. Mrs. Elphinstone thought they should try to board a train again, but my brother knew that would be hopeless. He said that they should make their way to the coast and leave the country altogether. The women agreed, and they turned the wagon eastward.

Along the way, the three travelers saw many people. There was a woman walking with two children and carrying a third, and a little cart crowded with children. Then a well-dressed man passed. He was looking at the ground and grabbing his own hair in a rage.

As they neared another town, Mrs. Elphinstone looked down the road and cried out, "Good heavens! What have you gotten us into?"

The three had come to a busy crossroads. The road across their path was filled with people, horses, and wagons of every sort. There were workmen, soldiers, railway porters, and farmers. Most wore ragged clothes. Some even wore the garments they had slept in. Carts and carriages were crowded wheel-to-wheel. Drivers hit their horses or yelled at other drivers. Every face had the same look of fear and pain. "Clear the way!" they cried. "Clear the way! The Martians are coming!"

My brother left the carriage and walked to the edge of the crowded road. Great clouds of dust and smoke hung in the air. A little girl stumbled from the road and sat down near my brother. He lifted her in his arms to put her in the carriage. Just then a woman cried out, "Ellen! Ellen!" The little girl shouted back, "Mother!" and sprang from my brother's arms.

An old man walked by clutching a small carrying case. As he passed my brother, the case split open and coins poured out onto the road. The man looked in horror as they rolled about on the ground. He threw himself to his knees, grabbing at the coins and stuffing handfuls into his pockets. Suddenly he disappeared from sight beneath a flurry of wheels and horses' hooves.

When the crowd cleared for a moment, the old man could be seen lying on the road, still clutching his money. My brother plunged into the traffic and grabbed the man's collar. He tried to drag him to safety, but the old man fought back.

Just then two wagons collided and the horses reared up around them. The old man twisted his head around and bit my brother's hand. There was nothing my brother could do but let go of him and jump back to the side of the road. As wagons and horses milled around him, the old man went back to gathering his coins. My brother returned to the two women, and the three of them tried to figure out a way around the moving wall of people and wagons. But they could think of none. To reach the coast, they would have to go through the mob.

While my brother approached the crossroads on foot, Miss Elphinstone took the reins and guided the carriage to the edge of the road. My brother darted into the traffic again and grabbed the horse that was pulling the wagon. Miss Elphinstone showed no fear and drove the carriage into the opening he had made. Once the carriage had made its way into the flow of travelers, he climbed back aboard and the trio slowly fought their way to the other side. It was a struggle, but finally they crossed over. They turned onto another roadway and left the crowded crossroads behind.

As the three travelers continued their journey eastward, they saw more fleeing crowds. Two trains rolled by in the distance, brimming with passengers. Finally they stopped, exhausted and hungry. Night fell, but the three travelers were too cold and too afraid to sleep.

CHAPTER 12

The *Thunder Child*

༄

There were gigantic, terrible stampedes on every road leading out of London. Six million people without food or water were trying to make their way out of the city. It was the beginning of the end of civilization—the end of humanity, really.

To the south of the city, everything grew blacker and blacker. From high above, the countryside must have looked like a sheet of paper being splashed with ink. The Martians were spreading their poison cloud closer and closer to London.

They destroyed any artillery they found, cut every telegraph line, and wrecked the train tracks. All the while, more cylinders fell from the sky.

In the heart of London, steamboats and ships of all sorts filled the River Thames. They were ready to take passengers to safety—for large sums of money. People who couldn't pay were not taken aboard—even when they swam out to the boats.

The black cloud caused panic as it floated down the river. Boats darted about in confusion at its approach. As they tried to escape, they kept colliding with one another. Desperate to avoid the cloud, people climbed down to the boats from the bridges above. The confusion grew even greater when a fighting-machine appeared near the Clock Tower and waded down the river. The Martians had reached the heart of London.

Meanwhile, people fleeing the city began to suffer from a lack of food. Farmers fought thieves to keep them from stealing crops and vegetables. Some people were so desperate and hungry that they headed back to London for food.

By Wednesday, my brother and the two women reached a town near the coast. When they got there, a group of people calling themselves the Committee of Public Supply took their horse. Then they forced the three travelers to continue on foot. Still, they pushed on until they reached the coast. The three looked out at the waters of the English Channel and were amazed to see ships of every size and kind. Boats could no longer reach London along the River Thames, so they had gathered up and down the coast instead. There were fishing vessels from many different countries, yachts, passenger ships, tankers, freighters, and a swarm of small boats carrying people from shore.

A couple of miles farther out was a warship—the *Thunder Child*. It was the only warship in sight, although great clouds of smoke on the horizon showed that others weren't far off. It looked as if they had formed a line across the mouth of the Thames and were ready to steam upriver.

At the sight of the channel, Mrs. Elphinstone became very upset. She had never been outside the country before, and the thought of leaving England made her fearful. She wanted nothing more than to return home to her husband. Miss Elphinstone calmed her sister-in-law. Then, with my brother's help, she managed to get the frightened woman down to the beach. There they paid thirty-six pounds to board a steamboat that would take them to safety.

Once aboard, they were able to regain some strength with a meal—although it, too, cost them dearly. In order to collect more money, the captain was taking on as many passengers as possible and did not leave right away. The boat grew more and more crowded until, at five o'clock, the sound of guns came echoing over the water from the south.

The warship—the *Thunder Child*—fired a small signal gun and raised its flags. Great clouds of smoke began to pour from its smokestacks. Meanwhile, the three warships that had been waiting out at sea quickly steamed into sight.

The captain of the steamboat grew angry at himself for not leaving sooner. He ordered his crew to stop taking on passengers and get under way. It was then that a Martian fighting-machine appeared. It was striding through the water from the south. All the passengers stood on deck and watched the distant shape get closer.

It was the first Martian my brother had seen. He stood amazed and terrified as it waded farther from land and closer to the boats. As they watched, another Martian appeared from behind some trees on shore. Then another, also headed for the sea. At the sight of the fighting-machines, the swarm of boats began their frantic escape. Whistles sounded and sails were let out. Boats turned wildly, nearly hitting one another. The steamboat was quickly at full speed, but even then it seemed to be standing still compared with the oncoming attackers.

The steamboat lurched to one side, and my brother was thrown to his knees. There was shouting all about him. Then he heard the rattle of feet running along the deck and a cheer from the passengers. He sprang to the railing and looked around just in time to see the *Thunder Child* speed by. Huge waves shot up from its bow, and fiery smoke poured from its twin stacks.

The three fighting-machines were now close together. They were standing so far out to sea that their tripod legs were almost completely under the waves. They seemed to be watching the *Thunder Child*, perhaps wondering what the thing was.

The warship steamed closer and closer to its targets. Suddenly one of the fighting-machines fired a shell of black gas. It hit the ship, but the *Thunder Child* sped safely through the poisonous cloud of black smoke that burst forth. Then one of the Martians raised its Heat-Ray and sent a beam into the water. As a great white cloud of steam sprang from the ocean, my brother saw a flicker of flame through the mist and heard the sound of the *Thunder Child*'s great guns. One of the Martians staggered under an explosion. It leaned first one way and then the other, and fell into the ocean in a great burst of water and smoke.

When they saw the Martian fall, everyone on the boats shouted wildly. They cheered even louder when they saw the warship emerge from the mist. It was headed for a second foe. The fighting-machine turned its Heat-Ray on its attacker. There was a blinding flash and a loud explosion from the *Thunder Child*. The Martian was rocked by the blast. Then it was struck by the warship and fell. Another great cheer rose up from all the ships and boats heading out to sea.

After that, my brother lost sight of the third Martian and the *Thunder Child*. There was too much smoke and steam from the battle to see what was happening. The other warships continued to move up and down the coast. Meanwhile the steamboat, along with all the other boats, headed out into the channel. They sailed toward the safety of Europe, where they would await the outcome of the battle.

The passengers looked back into the setting sun and heard the sound of guns coming from shore. As they watched their homeland get farther and farther away, a mass of black smoke appeared and hid the sunset from view.

Dusk had turned into night by the time the captain cried out and pointed to the sky. A dark shadow rushed up into the heavens. It flew above the clouds to the west. It was flat and broad and very large. My brother could only wonder what the thing was as he watched it sweep around in a curve, grow smaller, and finally disappear.

CHAPTER 13

Underfoot

∽

While my brother and his companions were escaping London, the curate and I were hiding in the deserted house. We were trapped by a cloud of black smoke that had surrounded us and cut us off from the world. I was worried about my wife and hoped that the Martians' march to London meant Leatherhead was safe. I was also becoming more upset with the curate. His fearfulness and lack of hope were tiring. I stayed away from him as much as possible, but he often followed me from room to room. Finally, I locked myself in the attic to escape his unhappiness.

At about midday on Monday, a Martian finally appeared. It was clearing the black smoke from fields and roads with a jet of steam. When it reached our house, the blast hissed against the walls and smashed all the windows. Later that afternoon, we dared to peer out again. The countryside looked as though a black snowstorm had passed over it. Everything was covered with a layer of black dust.

Seeing this, I was quite sure we could now escape. I guessed that the black smoke was harmless once it fell to the ground. I quickly gathered some food and water. The curate watched me and became more upset. "But we're safe here," he said. "We're safe . . ." Seeing that I was going to leave with or without him, he finally stopped muttering. And so, late in the afternoon, we crept from the house and took the blackened road in the direction of London. The work of the Martians lay all around us. Everything had been destroyed and sat burned or wrecked beneath a blanket of dust.

It wasn't until we reached the next town that we saw anyone else. People moved about looking for hiding places or food. Smashed wagons and bicycles lay scattered on the roads. As we crossed a bridge, I saw great red clumps floating down the river. They looked like some type of Martian plant.

Farther on, the curate and I saw a group of people running away. I could see a Martian fighting-machine above the rooftops behind them. It surely would have killed us if it had seen us. But it didn't, and the curate and I ran and hid in a shed.

We stayed there until twilight. The curate wanted to remain in the shed, but I was determined to find my wife, so we quietly hurried on.

We soon saw yet another Martian. It was walking across a field, chasing four or five people.

My companion and I hid in a ditch and waited until the Martian had gone. We crawled out under cover of darkness, staying off the roads and sneaking through bushes and fields until we came to another town. The curate complained that he was tired and thirsty, so we went into a house. We didn't find any food, but there was water to drink. I also took a hatchet, which I thought would be useful.

At the next house we found food—two loaves of bread, some steak, and half a ham. There was also canned soup, fish, crackers, and some beans. It was too dangerous to light a fire or lamp, so we sat in the darkness of the kitchen and ate our dinner.

Suddenly a blinding flash of green filled the room. A huge blow rocked the house. Broken glass, bricks, and plaster flew all around us. I was knocked across the floor and hit my head on the stove.

When I woke up, everything was dark. The curate was wiping my face with a wet cloth. His forehead glimmered with blood. "Are you all right?" he asked in a whisper. "You were out for a long time."

I told him I was fine and sat up.

"Don't move," he said. "The floor is covered with smashed glass and dishes. If you move, they might hear you."

We sat in silence. Everything was still except for the occasional sound of falling plaster or bricks. Outside I could hear a rattling, metal sound.

"What is it?" I asked.

The curate replied with wide, frightened eyes, "It's a Martian!"

We remained quiet for hours—until the dawn light slowly crept in. I thought that perhaps one of the fighting-machines had crashed into the house. But as it grew lighter, I could see that a great mound of dirt had knocked in the outside wall. The kitchen floor was littered with dishes, forks and knives, and broken furniture. The other walls were full of holes. Through them we could see that most of the building had been destroyed. A falling cylinder had struck the house.

As the morning grew brighter, we peered through a hole in the wall and saw a Martian standing guard over the pit made by the impact. We crawled away from the hole as quietly as possible and ran to a small room off the back of the kitchen. From the darkness of our new hiding place, we could hear hammering on metal, a loud hooting, and a hissing like the sound of an engine. These sounds were followed by a thudding noise. Then everything began to shake. For many hours, we sat there in the small, dark room, silent and shivering.

I must have fallen asleep at some point, because I woke up feeling very hungry. I crawled back into the kitchen as carefully as I could and found some food. The curate joined me, and we ate in silence.

CHAPTER 14

What We Saw from
the Ruined House

⌒

When we finished eating, the curate and I crept back into the small room behind the kitchen. I fell asleep again, and when I awoke, I was alone. I could still hear the thudding sound. I whispered for the curate and then crawled across the floor and looked in the kitchen. He was there, spying through the hole in the wall.

I carefully crawled over to my companion and touched him on the leg. He jumped in shock and knocked into some plaster, which fell with a loud noise. I held his arm and we sat frozen in fear. But the Martians hadn't heard us. I slid closer to the hole, looked out, and saw the destruction that had taken place.

The cylinder had wiped out the nearby houses. Its collision had made a large crater—larger than the one on Horsell Common. The cylinder lay at the bottom of this pit. The crash had also thrown dirt into the air. It had landed in piles all around the pit, burying the wrecked homes. The house we were in was almost completely gone. Only the kitchen and the small room in which we were hiding remained. These two rooms were buried under tons of rubble. Only the side facing the cylinder was uncovered. There we sat, hanging on the edge of the pit, overlooking the Martians.

The cylinder was lying open in the center of the crater. One of the fighting machines stood nearby. It was empty, but still looked tall against the evening sky. Moving about beside the cylinder was something I had never seen before. It looked like a metal spider with five legs. Its body was covered with levers and mechanical tentacles. As I watched, the tentacles reached into the cylinder, pulled out a number of metal rods, plates, and bars, and placed them on the ground. It was using these to build another device like itself. The handling-machine moved swiftly—as if it were alive.

That was when I noticed the Martians. One was controlling the handling-machine while the others moved slowly about nearby. I had seen the creatures on Horsell Common, but this was my first chance to see the things close up. I now saw that the alien's V-shaped mouth was more like a bird's beak. On the back of the head—or body—was an opening covered with skin. It looked like the top of a drum, and I guessed that this was the creature's ear. Clustered around the mouth were two bunches of eight tentacles. The bunches reminded me of a pair of hands. The Martians crawled slowly and painfully along the ground, pushing and pulling themselves about with these limbs.

Watching them, I saw that the invaders were much more advanced than humans. We may have our bicycles, wagons, boats—even our gliding-machines—but they had their cylinders, their fighting and handling-machines, their Heat-Rays, and their cannons. It was as if they were brains without bodies. They just built whatever mechanical bodies they needed.

I also noticed that their machines did not use wheels or levers. Instead, they were powered by devices that I would describe as mechanical muscles. These muscles moved the Martian machines the same way our muscles move our bodies. It is no wonder their machines looked and moved so much like animals.

There were other ways in which the invaders

were different from us as well. From my hiding place in the house, I watched the Martians closely and saw groups of four, five, or six of them working together on a difficult task. They made no sounds and did nothing with their tentacles to make me think they were signaling one another. But I am sure they were communicating. In fact, I am convinced that they could read one another's thoughts.

I also watched a small digging-machine at work. It crawled around the pit like a metal crab, making the hole larger and giving off jets of green gas as it went. As I looked at the machines quickly going about their work and the sluggish, clumsy Martians, I had to remind myself that it was the Martians who were the living creatures, not the machines.

As I was peering through the hole, a second fighting-machine appeared. This was followed by others carrying still more devices that I had never seen before. The second handling-machine was completed and it operated one of these new devices. The new machine looked like a metal drum with a funnel on top. The funnel turned slowly, powered by one tentacle of the handling-machine. With two other tentacles, the handling-machine fed dirt into the funnel. A white powder flowed out of the funnel and into a pan.

The handling-machine took the white powder and placed it in yet another device. Finally, using another tentacle, the handling-machine removed a shining bar of metal from the last machine. This was then placed on a growing stack on one side of the pit. In a matter of minutes, the handling-machine, the drum-shaped machine, and the third device had turned dirt and clay into a polished piece of metal. I was sure the Martians planned to make more machines from this metal.

CHAPTER 15

The Death of the Curate

⟋⟍

As the days passed, the curate and I remained trapped in the house. The only thing we could do was watch the Martians build their machines. As our hunger and exhaustion grew, so did my impatience with my companion.

I had never liked the curate's sense of helplessness. While I did everything I could to survive, he could only complain that anything we did was useless. Instead of helping, he would cry for hours. He ate more than I did, even when I told him we needed to make our food last. While the

Martians worked outside, we began to argue and fight in our dark hole.

I spent hours trying to figure out a way to escape. The curate, of course, was no help. I thought we might be able to dig our way out, so I tried making a tunnel with my hatchet. Unfortunately, the tunnel quickly collapsed. When this failed, I decided that it was best to just wait. I knew that the Martians would eventually leave their cylinders to do battle. Once they were gone, we would be free of our prison.

On the sixth day of hiding in the house, I was looking through the hole in the wall when I realized I was alone. I quietly went back into the small room and found the curate drinking a bottle of water. He had been eating and drinking too much again, so I grabbed the bottle from his hand. We struggled, and the bottle fell to the floor and broke. In the darkness of the small room, we stood facing each other angrily.

I sat down between the curate and the food, and told him we would have to make our supplies last. Then I told him he couldn't eat anything else that day. I knew I couldn't trust him alone, so hour after hour we faced each other grimly. I was tired, but I had made up my mind. Of course, he cried and complained of hunger the whole time.

We fought whenever the curate tried to get at the food. When we weren't fighting, I tried to convince him that I was right. I even offered the last bottle of water to calm him, but nothing worked. He kept trying to get to the food. Finally, he started talking nonsense. He had gone mad.

On the eighth day, the curate began to talk in a loud voice instead of a whisper. "We deserve this," he said. "Humans have done so many bad things. That's why the Martians are attacking." Then he begged me for food again. I refused, and he got angry. He said that he would shout out to the Martians so they would find us, but I didn't give in. He kept up this behavior until night came and he fell asleep.

The next day, he began to yell loudly again. "Be quiet!" I commanded, rising to my feet.

"No! I can't take this anymore," he wailed. He bolted from our hiding place and ran into the kitchen. By the time I reached the doorway, the curate was gone. He must have scrambled through the hole in the wall and into the pit. I was certain that the Martians had captured him.

Suddenly I heard a noise from outside. A dark shadow moved across the hole. I looked up and saw the underside of a handling-machine slide across the opening. One of the machine's arms reached in, followed by another. I stood motionless with fear. A piece of glass appeared over the hole. Through the glass, the large dark eyes of a Martian peered in. A long metal tentacle snaked its way into the room. I watched as it twisted this way and that.

I slowly turned and made my way from the kitchen. Back in the small room, I listened as the tentacle moved about. Every now and then it tapped against a wall. It gave off a faint metallic sound as it moved.

There was a coal cellar off the small room. I opened the door to it and squeezed inside. I covered myself with firewood and coal as quietly as I could.

The tentacle moved about in the kitchen until it reached the entrance to the small room. It entered, hovered closer, and hung in the air just beyond my hiding place. I heard it fumbling at the latch. The Martians understood doors!

The tentacle slowly opened the door to the coal cellar. In the darkness, I saw it moving about like an elephant's trunk—swaying back and forth. When it touched the heel of my boot, I nearly screamed. Then I heard the clicking sound of the thing grabbing at something. I thought it had me, but instead it grasped a piece of coal and disappeared with it back into the kitchen.

Then the tentacle reached into the small room a second time. I was sure that it would find me at last, but instead it clutched the coal cellar door and closed it. It pulled itself back into the

kitchen and knocked some cans and bottles about. After that came silence.

I knew it was probably gone, but I did not crawl from my hiding place for more than a day. I went without food and water for all that time. It wasn't until the eleventh day in the house that I felt it was safe enough for me to come out.

CHAPTER 16

Stillness

～

As soon as I pulled myself from the coal cellar, I crawled into the kitchen and went in search of something to eat and drink. The food that the curate and I had saved was gone. The Martian must have taken it all. And so I had nothing. By the twelfth day, my throat hurt so much that I pumped a glassful of blackened rainwater from the water pump. I knew the sound could give me away, but I had to have a drink.

On the fourteenth day, I crept into the kitchen and was surprised to see that a red weed had grown over the hole in the wall. It made the entire room glow a bloodred color.

The next day, I heard a sound in the kitchen. I listened for a moment and realized that it was a dog. When I went into the kitchen, the dog saw me and barked. I tried to get closer, but it turned and ran through the red growth over the hole. It was then that I noticed the pit was quiet. I listened carefully. All I could hear were birds fluttering about and the dog running back and forth.

I carefully looked out through the curtain of red plants. In one corner of the crater, a large flock of crows was eating something that lay on the ground. Except for the birds and the dog, there wasn't a living thing in the pit.

I looked around, unable to believe my eyes. The Martians and their machines were gone. I pulled myself through the hole and stood on a mound of rubble. Then I scrambled to the edge of the pit. There was not a single Martian in sight.

I turned my attention to my surroundings. What I saw left me stunned. It looked as if I had been transported to another planet.

Where there had been streets lined with houses and trees, there was now nothing but bricks, clay, and gravel. Red cactus-like plants were growing everywhere. Trees hung lifeless, covered with a thick layer of Martian plant life. Red weeds grew on whatever remained of the wrecked houses.

I felt like a rabbit returning home to find humans building a house over my burrow. I understood now that humans had lost their place on Earth. From here on, we were animals just like all the other animals. The Martians were the masters. Our fate was now to run and hide the way animals ran from us.

After a time, my hunger forced me to abandon these thoughts. I left the pit in search of food.

As I walked, I saw the red weed growing everywhere. It had sprung up so quickly along the rivers that it turned the waterways into a mass of red. Finally I found a small patch of garden that wasn't buried by the red weeds. Here I gathered some onions and carrots. I also came upon a patch of grass where I found some mushrooms. I ate all of them hungrily.

The farther I went, the fewer weeds I saw. There were wrecked buildings, but there were also places where the houses were untouched. Some looked as if there could have been people living inside. I went in some of the houses to hunt for food, but it was all gone. I was too tired to push on, so I rested for the remainder of the day.

After sunset, I continued on my way. I saw signs of the Heat-Ray everywhere, but I saw no people and no sign of the Martians. I was starting to believe that humanity was gone and that I was the last man alive. I thought for sure we had been wiped out and that the invaders had taken over the entire country. For all I knew, they were destroying Berlin or Paris at that very moment.

CHAPTER 17

The Man on Putney Hill

∽

I spent my first night away from the wrecked house at an inn. It was the first time I'd slept in a bed since my wife and I had escaped to Leatherhead, but I did not sleep well. It wasn't until much later that night that my mind cleared and I thought about everything that had happened.

I was haunted by the death of the curate. If I had known how things would turn out, I never would have stayed with him for so long. But when I thought about everything he had done, I realized that there was no way I could have known how it would end. There was nothing that I could have done.

I also thought about my wife and wondered if she was still alive. I imagined a hundred different things that could have happened to her. With these thoughts going through my mind, it turned into a long, terrible night.

But the next morning was bright and clear, and the eastern sky glowed pink. I was on the outskirts of London by now, but I decided I would go to Leatherhead instead. I knew there was little chance that my wife would still be there. If she was alive, she and my cousins would have fled the approaching Martians. But even if they were gone, it was there that I would begin my search. All I knew was that I missed her and had to find her.

I set out and saw right away that the roads were filled with signs of panic and flight. There was a cart with a smashed wheel, a straw hat trampled into the mud, and an overturned water trough. At Putney Hill, I came upon a swampy place among some trees and saw a swarm of little frogs. I stopped to look at them. If they could survive all of this, I thought, perhaps there was still hope.

The tiny creatures hopped away, and I suddenly had the feeling that I was being watched. I turned and saw someone hiding in a clump of bushes. It was a man. I took a step toward him, and he stood up. His clothes were as dusty and filthy as mine. His black hair hung over his eyes, and his face was dirty. I could see he was carrying a sword.

"Stop," he shouted. "Where do you come from?"

"I was trapped in a house when a cylinder landed," I said and pointed in the direction I had come from. "But I escaped."

"There's no food here," he said sternly. "This area is mine. There is only food for one."

"I'm not stopping," I said. "I'm on my way to Leatherhead to find my wife."

He raised his hand and pointed at me. "It's you," he said in surprise. "The man from Maybury. You weren't killed at Weybridge!"

Suddenly I recognized him. It was the artilleryman who had come into my garden. "I lost you when the Martians attacked by the river," I said.

He motioned for me to crawl under some bushes where we could talk without being seen. Once we were safely under cover, I asked him what he knew. "Toward the south, the sky is bright with the light from the Martians," he replied. "It's like a city. The night before last, I saw something in the air. I think they've built a flying-machine . . ."

I was stunned at this news. "A flying-machine?" I said. "Then it's all over. If they can fly, they can go around the world."

He looked at me. "Yes, it is all over. But I knew that already. After all, in all this time, how many have we destroyed? They've walked all over us. And they just keep coming. Those green falling stars—I haven't seen any for five or six days, but I'm sure they're falling somewhere else. This isn't a war," he said. "It was never any more of a war than the war between men and ants."

He went on. "Once they take over, the Martians will have an easy time of it with most people. The ones with no fighting spirit. The ones who are used to going to work, coming home, doing the same thing every day, and then going to church every Sunday. Life under the Martians won't be that different for them. They'll live in cages and they'll be fed."

"No," I cried, "that's impossible. No human beings would let themselves . . ." But I could see that he might be right. "What are you going to do?" I asked.

119

"Well, I've been thinking," he replied. "I believe we can live underground in the sewers. I know it sounds terrible, but there are hundreds of miles of sewers beneath the streets of London. And with no one living in the city, they'll be clean after just a few days' rain. The main sewers are big enough. Then there are cellars, underground vaults, railway tunnels, and subways. You see? We gather a group of strong men and women. No weak ones. We can't have them. Then the human race can go on.

"But saving humanity isn't enough. We must save our knowledge, too. And add to it. Otherwise we're no better than rats. We must find safe places deep beneath the city and get all the books we can. We have to go to the British Museum and go through the books. But we don't want any useless novels or poetry—just our science and ideas.

"And we have to watch the Martians—watch them, but leave them alone. Show them we mean no harm. They're intelligent. They won't hunt us down if they have all they want and think we're harmless.

"And then, just think. What if we were able to capture four or five of their fighting-machines? Imagine being in control of their Heat-Ray. Imagine the Martians on the run and humans fighting back!"

I had not thought that far into the future, but what the artilleryman said made sense. We talked more about his plan as we made our way to the house where he had been hiding. However, when I saw the tunnel he was digging in the cellar of the house, I began to have doubts. He had been working at it for a week, yet the tunnel was only ten yards deep. I could have dug that in a day. No matter what his plan might be, I began to wonder if he was the man to carry it out.

Still, we took up shovels and started digging. It felt good to be working at something—to have a purpose. Later that morning, however, my doubts returned. I wondered why we had to dig a tunnel at all when we could climb down into the sewers through a manhole. And why were we digging from this house when there were other houses closer to the sewer?

Around midday, the artilleryman turned to me and said, "Let's take a break. I think it's time we went to the roof to see what's going on."

We went upstairs and peered out of a door on the rooftop. We didn't see any Martians, so we climbed out on the roof and hid under an overhang. From our hiding place we could see the river—a ribbon of red—and trees covered in creeping red plants. In the distance, black smoke was rising. There was a blue haze all around us.

The artilleryman began to talk about his plans again. He spoke so confidently that I almost began to believe in him once more. But

I knew by now that it would not happen. He would not be the one to capture or fight the great machines.

After a while, we went down to the cellar. We didn't feel like digging, so we ate. The artilleryman was in a good mood and was glad that we had found each other again. We both relaxed, and he brought out some cards and a chessboard. It was strange. While humanity was nearing its end, we were sitting in the cellar playing games.

After our games, I went up to the roof again. To the west, the hills were hidden in shadow. In the distance, fires glowed red. In the sky, Mars was red and clear. It shone high above the horizon.

It was then that I decided to leave the artilleryman. I felt badly for wasting my time with him instead of searching for my wife and trying to find out what the Martians were doing.

I thought about what I should do. I decided there would be nothing left to find in Leatherhead, so I made up my mind to go on to London instead. Perhaps there I would find help or find out what had happened to my wife.

CHAPTER 18

Dead London

⁓

That night, I left the artilleryman. I crossed the river over a bridge nearly choked with red weed. I noticed that patches of white had begun to appear on the alien plant. It was being killed by bacteria, which the plant could not resist. In some places, the Martian weed had shriveled, become brittle, and fallen off.

Beyond the bridge, a thick layer of black dust covered the quiet streets. The shops were closed and the houses locked up. Everything was quiet. Here and there, people had broken into homes or shops. The window of a jewelry store was smashed. Gold chains and a watch lay on the floor. Then I came upon a row of houses that were on fire. The city had been so deadly quiet that I was glad to hear even the sound of the burning homes.

The closer I got to the heart of London, the quieter the city became. Then suddenly I heard a howling. At first it was very low and distant—two notes over and over. *Ulla, ulla, ulla, ulla.* It sounded lonely and full of fear.

The sound grew louder as I moved closer to it. It made me feel tired and afraid. When I thought about my wife and friends, it made me feel alone.

As the sun was setting, I found myself at the gates of a large park. I gazed beyond some far-off trees and saw the hood of a fighting-machine. The howling sound was coming from this Martian. I watched for a while, but it didn't move. I couldn't see why the Thing was standing and making such a sound. More curious than afraid now, I made my way around the park for a closer look.

I came upon a wrecked handling-machine near a train station. It was lying in the ruins of a house. Its tentacles were smashed and twisted. The machine looked as if it had crashed into the building.

I pushed on and soon saw a second fighting-machine in another park. It was standing as motionless as the first. At that moment, the distant wail of *Ulla, ulla . . .* stopped. The sudden silence was as startling as a thunderclap.

By now, the sun had set. The houses around me were dark, and the trees in the park were growing black. The windows in the houses were like eye sockets in skulls. As the city grew darker, I grew more afraid. I began to imagine a thousand dangers moving around me. I ran until I found shelter in an empty shack, where I spent the night.

My courage returned just before dawn, and I decided to explore some more. After walking for a short time, I found myself at the bottom of a small hill. At the top of the hill, towering up to the fading stars, was a third Martian. It, too, was motionless. At the sight of the machine, I think I gave up all hope. I no longer cared what happened to me and marched desperately toward the Martian.

As I got closer, I saw a huge flock of black birds flying about the fighting-machine's head. My heart leaped and I began running. I realized that something must have happened to the Martians. I hurried through the red weed that lay around me and ran up the slope. Great mounds of dirt formed the rim of a pit at the feet of the machine. The thought that had flashed into my mind grew stronger. I felt no fear as I ran up the hill toward the motionless machine.

I scrambled up the mounds of earth and looked into the pit. Machines lay here and there in the large hole. Scattered about in overturned fighting-machines or lying on the ground were the Martians—*dead*! Nearly fifty creatures lay motionless in the shadows below. A dozen lay neatly in a row. These things that had been alive and so terrible to humans were now dead.

I realized that they had been killed in the same way that the red weeds had been destroyed. They had been killed by earthly bacteria against which they had no defense. After all of our guns and warships had failed to stop them, the Martians had been brought down by the smallest living things on our planet.

Since the beginning of life on Earth, germs have caused illness and death in all living things. After enough time passed, however, we grew resistant to most of them. But as we have now discovered, there are no bacteria on Mars. When the Martians came to Earth, these earthly germs began to fight their own war against the invaders.

Even if the Martians had been ten times stronger, they still would have been defeated.

As the sunrise lit up the city, I stood staring into the crater. The Martians' strange devices, so powerful and so much more advanced than ours, lay in the shadows. On the other side of the pit was their great flying-machine. The crows cawed loudly, and I looked up at the huge fighting-machine that would fight no more.

From the top of the hill, I could see the other two fighting-machines. They, too, were lifeless and still. I could also see the great city of London stretched out before me. I looked at the houses and factories and churches, silent and abandoned. I thought of the people who called London home and of the destruction the city had suffered. Tears came to my eyes at the thought of this dead city coming to life again.

The torment was over. The healing would begin. The survivors scattered over the country and the thousands who had fled by sea would begin to return. The pulse of life would grow stronger and stronger. The invaders had been stopped. All of the ruins would soon be rebuilt.

Then, in a great wave of emotion, I thought of what I had just been through. And I thought of my wife and the life we had known, which was now gone forever.

CHAPTER 19

Wreckage

◦◦◦

I was not the first to discover the end of the
Martian threat. Not long after I'd left the wrecked
house, someone else had seen that the Martians
were dying and managed to send a telegraph to
Paris. From there, the news quickly spread all
over the world. While I was standing at the edge
of the pit, people in a thousand cities around the
world were already crying with joy. Trains were
being readied to return to London. Church bells
across England were beginning to ring. Boats
with food of every kind were speeding to our

shores from across the English Channel, the Irish Sea, and the Atlantic Ocean. All the ships in the world seemed to be heading to London.

But I did not know of any of this. And I don't remember anything after making my discovery. I must have wandered from the pit, half out of my mind. When I finally came to my senses, I was in bed in the home of a family who had taken me in. They had found me wandering, weeping and raving through the streets. They said I was singing some strange song about being the last man alive.

After I told them my story, they told me what they had heard about Leatherhead. The town had been destroyed while I was hiding in the house with the curate. A Heat-Ray had swept it out of existence.

I stayed with the family for four days, until I felt a growing need to go home. They didn't think it was a good idea, but I had to go. I promised I would return and went out into the streets again.

Unlike my mood, the day was bright. Some shops were open, and the streets were already busy with people. I even saw a drinking fountain that was working again. Londoners were everywhere. They were busy putting their world back in order. It was hard to believe that anything had happened. But then I looked closely and saw that everyone appeared tired and hungry. People's hair was dirty and ragged. Many wore torn and filthy clothes. The expressions on their faces were grim.

Trains had started to run again, and I boarded one at Waterloo station. As we headed south, I watched the blackened ruins through my window. It had rained for two days, but the powder of the black smoke still lay on the ground. The track had been wrecked in many places. The train rocked back and forth as it traveled on rails that had just been fixed.

Every little stream was a heaped mass of red weed. Along the way, I saw piles of dirt from the

135

pit that held the sixth cylinder. A crowd of people gathered around it. Someone had raised a British flag at the site. It waved in the morning breeze.

The track outside Woking was still being repaired, so I left the train and continued on foot. I walked past where the artilleryman and I had talked to the soldiers and by the spot where I had seen the Martian in the thunderstorm. I made my way through the woods, past the Spotted Dog, and finally arrived home.

The front door had been knocked in. It swung back and forth in the breeze. As soon as I entered, I felt the emptiness of the place. Muddy footsteps still trailed up the stairs. In the dining room, spoiled food sat on the table where the artilleryman and I had left it. Any hope I had that my wife would greet me disappeared.

And then I heard a voice say, "It's no use. The house is deserted. No one has been here in days."

I turned, walked to the doors that opened to the garden, and looked out. There, amazed and afraid, were my cousin and my wife. She saw me and gave a faint cry.

"I knew," she said looking at me. "I knew . . ."

She put her hand to her mouth. I took a step forward and caught her in my arms.

CHAPTER 20

Epilogue

ᘓ

Now that we have examined the bodies of the Martians, we know the creatures are made up mostly of their brains. They have huge nerves leading to the eyes, ears, and tentacles. They also have hearts, lungs, and a few other organs, but these are only a small part of their bodies. Unlike humans, the Martians do not eat. Instead, they use the blood of other living things to replace their own. In each cylinder, we found the remains of odd, two-legged creatures that must have provided the Martians with food on their journey. To us, this seems horrible. But is it any more horrible than humans eating other animals? It even makes sense when you think about how much of our body is used to eat and digest food, and how much energy we spend doing that. Martian bodies have developed beyond that.

We discovered that the Martians are different from humans in other ways, too. They do not sleep because they don't have the same need to rest. They don't have offspring the way humans do, either. In fact, we now know that an infant Martian was born on Earth during the war. It was found attached to its parent, like a bud growing from an adult plant.

As strange as this all sounds, some people think that humans could become like Martians in the distant future. They think that with the passage of enough time, we will build machines to do the work of our arms and legs. They also think that we will one day feed ourselves as the

Martians do. Some imagine a far-off time when most of the human body will be replaced by an immense brain. The only other part of the body that would grow large would be the hands. Perhaps our hands would grow to look like the Martians' tentacles. Perhaps, long ago, Martians didn't look so different from humans.

Scientists still don't know what the black smoke is made of—although they think something in the smoke works like a poison that attacks human blood. They have been trying to figure out how the Heat-Ray works, but there have been terrible accidents in the laboratories, and the work has stopped for now.

A more important question remains. Will the Martians return? The truth is, I don't think we're doing enough to find an answer. Every time Mars's orbit carries it close to Earth, I believe another attack could come. It would be easy enough to watch the planet carefully for signs of the next invasion. Then we could destroy the cylinders while the Martians are still inside. Or we could kill them as they crawl out, before they have time to build their machines. Now that we know they could attack again, it seems to me that their victory is very unlikely. They won't be able to surprise us again. Perhaps that's why they haven't returned—because they know they have lost their chance.

There are some who think the Martians have landed on Venus. Seven months ago, the orbits of Venus and Mars carried them close to each other. Shortly after this, strange markings appeared on the surfaces of both planets. Some think the markings may have been a signal from one planet to the other.

Whether they invade again or not, the Martians have changed our understanding of the future. We now know we are not entirely safe on our planet. We can never be sure what dangers lie out there in space. They have given us warning that we cannot spend too much of our time on wasteful and useless activities as we go about our daily lives. And they have shown us that no matter what country we are from, we all belong to a single race—the human race.

We also know now that if they can reach Earth, we can someday travel through space as well. And when the slow cooling of the sun makes life on Earth impossible, we will be able to leave our planet for another. Perhaps it won't be long before humans travel to the other planets and make them our new homes. Then again, perhaps the Martians will return and they, not us, will ultimately rule the solar system.

As I write this, it is easy for me to look out my study window and imagine the countryside in flames. When I walk along the streets, I see myself hurrying from hiding place to hiding place with the artilleryman. I see the black powder darkening the roadways. And then I wake, cold and scared, in the dark of the night.

It is strange to stand on Primrose Hill now and look out at the houses stretching to the horizon. It is strange to see crowds of sightseers stopping to look at the Martian machine still standing there. And it is strange to hear the laughter of children playing where I stood on that day—the last day of the war of the worlds.

What Do *You* Think?
Questions for Discussion

❦

Have you ever been around a toddler who keeps asking the question "Why?" Does your teacher call on you in class with questions from your homework? Do your parents ask you questions about your day at the dinner table? We are always surrounded by questions that need a specific response. But is it possible to have a question with no right answer?

The following questions are about the book you just read. But this is not a quiz! They are designed to help you look at the people, places, and events in the story from different angles. These questions do not have specific answers. Instead, they might make you think of the story in a completely new way.

Think carefully about each question and enjoy discovering more about this classic story.

In this story, the Martians come to Earth and try to take over the planet.

1. Do you believe in aliens? If they exist, do you think they would be friendly or hostile?

2. The author says that difficult conditions may have made the Martians crueler and more desperate to stay alive. Do you think the same would be true of humans? What is the most difficult position you've ever found yourself in?

3. The narrator says, "As scared as I was, I also wanted to get a closer look at the Martians." Why do you think he feels this way? Would you have stayed to look at the creatures or run away? What's the scariest thing that has ever happened to you?

4. Why do you suppose the narrator insists on going home instead of staying in Leatherhead like his wife wants? Have you ever done anything that someone asked you not to do?

5. On his way out of London, the narrator's brother stops to save two young women. Do you think this was a brave or a stupid thing to do? What is the bravest thing you've ever done?

6. While the narrator does all he can to survive, the curate does nothing but complain and cry. Do you know anyone like either of these men? Which of them are you more like?

7. When the Martians enter the house where the narrator is staying, the narrator hides in the coal cellar. Do you think this was a good hiding place? Where do you hide when you don't want to be found?

8. The artilleryman says, "Saving humanity isn't enough. We must save our knowledge, too. . . . But we don't want any useless novels or

poetry—just our science and ideas." Why do you suppose he feels this way? What would you choose to save?

9. When the narrator realizes that the fight is over, he says, "The torment was over. The healing would begin." Do you think the people of London can ever truly heal from the effects of the invasion? Has anything ever happened to you that caused a big change in your life?

10. At the beginning of the book, the narrator is sure that the military can easily destroy the Martians. How does his opinion change throughout the book? Were you surprised that something as small as bacteria finally killed them? How did you expect the story to end?

Afterword
by Arthur Pober, Ed.D.

⌒

First impressions are important.

Whether we are meeting new people, going to new places, or picking up a book unknown to us, first impressions count for a lot. They can lead to warm, lasting memories or can make us shy away from any future encounters.

Can you recall your own first impressions and earliest memories of reading the classics?

Do you remember wading through pages and pages of text to prepare for an exam? Or were you the child who hid under the blanket to read with a flashlight, joining forces with Robin Hood to save Maid Marian? Do you remember only how long it took you to read a lengthy novel such as *Little Women*? Or did you become best friends with the March sisters?

Even for a gifted young reader, getting through long chapters with dense language can easily become overwhelming and can obscure the richness of the story and its characters. Reading an abridged, newly crafted version of a classic novel can be the gentle introduction a child needs to explore the characters and storyline without the frustration of difficult vocabulary and complex themes.

Reading an abridged version of a classic novel gives the young reader a sense of independence and the satisfaction of finishing a "grown-up" book. And when a child is engaged with and inspired by a classic story, the tone is set for further exploration of the story's themes, characters, history, and details. As a child's reading skills advance, the desire to tackle the original, unabridged version of the story will naturally emerge.

If made accessible to young readers, these stories can become invaluable tools for understanding themselves in the context of their families and social environments. This is why the Classic Starts series includes questions that stimulate discussion regarding the impact and social relevance of the characters and stories today. These questions can foster lively conversations between children and their parents or teachers. When we look at the issues, values, and standards of past times in terms of how we live now, we can appreciate literature's classic tales in a very personal and engaging way.

Share your love of reading the classics with a young child, and introduce an imaginary world real enough to last a lifetime.

Dr. Arthur Pober, Ed.D.

Dr. Arthur Pober has spent more than twenty years in the fields of early childhood and gifted education. He is the former principal of one of the world's oldest laboratory schools for gifted youngsters, Hunter College Elementary School, and former Director of Magnet Schools for the Gifted and Talented for more than 25,000 youngsters in New York City.

Dr. Pober is a recognized authority in the areas of media and child protection and is currently the U.S. representative to the European Institute for the Media and European Advertising Standards Alliance.

Explore these wonderful stories in our
Classic Starts™ library.

Oliver Twist

Pollyanna

The Prince and the Pauper

Rebecca of Sunnybrook Farm

The Red Badge of Courage

Robinson Crusoe

The Secret Garden

The Story of King Arthur and His Knights

The Strange Case of Dr. Jekyll and Mr. Hyde

The Swiss Family Robinson

The Three Musketeers

Treasure Island

The War of the Worlds

White Fang

The Wind in the Willows